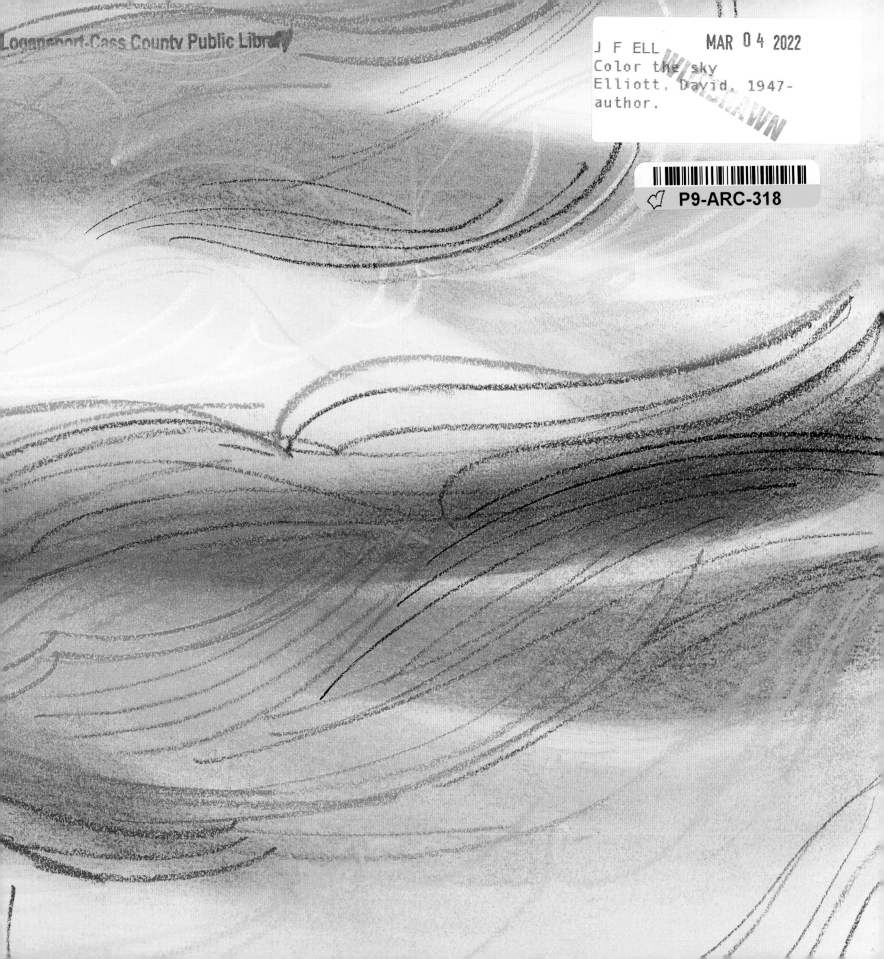

COLOR the SKY

Words by DAVID ELLIOTT • Art by EVAN TURK

LB

LITTLE, BROWN AND COMPANY

New York Boston

To Susan Goodman, my smart, funny friend
—DE

For Stephen, Laura, and Graham
—ET

Red big.

Red small.

Red sits on my
garden wall.

Blue low.

Blue high.

Blue has taken to the sky.

Black

is drinking

from my cup.

White has flown away.

Yellow sings,
"Wake up! Wake up!"

Green shouts, "Come and play!"

Brown left.

Brown right.

Brown in shadow.
Brown in light.

Orange here.

Orange there.

Orange disappears
in leaf and air...

And bursts
into an orange song.

Then all the colors
sing along.

Purple joins the chorus, too.
She's with her cousins,
Red and Blue.

Color!
Color!

On the wing!

and sing.

and sing

and sing

They sing

And I sing with them,
clear and light.

And spread my wings...

And take flight.

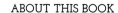

ABOUT THIS BOOK

The illustrations for this book were done in pastel and charcoal on drawing paper. This book was edited by Esther Cajahuaringa and Andrea Spooner and designed by Patrick Collins with art direction from Saho Fujii. The production was supervised by Bernadette Flinn, and the production editor was Annie McDonnell. The text was set in Josefin Slab, and the display type is Potato Cut.

• Little, Brown and Company • Hachette Book Group • 1290 Avenue of the Americas, New York, NY 10104 • Visit us at LBYR.com • First Edition: February 2022 • Little, Brown and Company is a division of Hachette Book Group, Inc. • The Little, Brown name and logo are trademarks of Hachette Book Group, Inc. • The publisher is not responsible for websites (or their content) that are not owned by the publisher. • Library of Congress Cataloging-in-Publication Data • Names: Elliott, David, 1947- author. | Turk, Evan, illustrator. • Title: Color the sky / words by David Elliott ; art by Evan Turk. • Description: First edition. | New York : Little, Brown and Company, 2022. | Audience: Ages 4-8. | Summary: "A story that celebrates the many colors of birds and the wonder of first flight"– Provided by publisher. • Identifiers: LCCN 2021006278 | ISBN 9780316212076 (hardcover) • Subjects: CYAC: Stories in rhyme. | Birds—Fiction. | Flight—Fiction. | Color—Fiction. • Classification: LCC PZ8.3.E492 Co 2022 | DDC [E]—dc23 • LC record available at https://lccn.loc.gov/2021006278 • ISBN 978-0-316-21207-6 • PRINTED IN CHINA • APS •

10 9 8 7 6 5 4 3 2 1